The
STORYTELLER

Story and Pictures

by

Elizabeth Koda-Callan

WORKMAN PUBLISHING, NEW YORK

The design/logo, including the words "Elizabeth Koda-Callan's Magic Charm
Books," is a registered trademark of Elizabeth Koda-Callan.
"Magic Charm Books" and "Elizabeth Koda-Callan's Magic Charm Books" are
trademarks of Elizabeth Koda-Callan.
Cover illustration by Elizabeth Koda-Callan.

Library of Congress Cataloging-in-Publication Data

Koda-Callan, Elizabeth.
The storyteller/ by Elizabeth Koda-Callan.
p. cm.
Summary: A little girl who cannot succeed in any of the activities at summer camp
finds her place when she shares her love of books and reading with the others
at the nightly campfire.
ISBN 0-7611-0535-2
[1.Camps—Fiction. 2. Books and reading—Fiction. 3. Self-acceptance—Fiction.]
I. Title. II. Series: Koda-Callan, Elizabeth. Elizabeth Koda-Callan's magic charm books.
PZ7.K8175St   1996
[E]—dc20
96-21307
CIP
AC

Workman books are available at special discounts when purchased in bulk
for premiums and sales promotions, as well as for fund-raising or educational use.
Special editions or book excerpts can also be created to specification.
For details, contact the Special Sales Director at the address below.

Workman Publishing Company, Inc.
708 Broadway
New York, NY 10003-9555
Printed in China
First printing October 1996
10 9 8 7 6 5 4 3 2 1

For Jennifer Callan
and
Barbara Hegedüs

Once there was a little girl who loved to read. She especially enjoyed the excitement of a great adventure—and often imagined herself as the heroine.

One day the little girl was reading a book to her mother. It was a story about summer camp. When she was finished, her mother suggested that the little girl might be ready for an adventure of her own.

"How would you like to go to sleep-away camp this summer?" her mother asked.

The little girl thought for a moment. "It sounds like it might be fun. O.K.," she said.

The little girl soon received a brochure with pictures of the camp as well as a long list of things she should bring along with her. She was very excited, but she was also beginning to wonder. *What if I don't like camp? What if I don't make any friends?* she thought. So when it came time to pack, she put some of her favorite books into her duffle bag—just in case.

Before she knew it, the big day arrived. As the bus pulled up in front of the house, the little girl kissed her mother and father good-bye. She slowly boarded the bus, then turned and smiled as bravely as she could.

The bus was filled with excited children talking quietly among themselves. The little girl was feeling shy, so she sat by herself and stared out the window.

After a long ride, the bus turned onto a winding gravel road. There were deep pine woods on both sides. Through the trees, the little girl could see the camp set on the edge of a beautiful lake. It looked exactly like the pictures in the brochure.

The little girl met the other campers and the counselor assigned to her group. The counselor took them all to the cabin they would be sharing. "Take some time to unpack and get acquainted," she said. "Then meet me outside for a game of volleyball."

The other girls unpacked quickly and went to meet the counselor. But the little girl lingered behind. She didn't think she liked volleyball. So instead she took out one of her books, settled into her bed and began to read.

Soon she was so engrossed in the story that she completely forgot where she was.

Suddenly she heard footsteps. The little girl looked up and was startled to see her counselor standing there. "I'm surprised you're still here," said the counselor. "Everyone's outside playing. Is anything wrong?"

"I don't think I'm very good at volleyball," answered the little girl.

"It doesn't matter how good you are. It's still fun. Why don't you give it a try?"

The little girl and her counselor walked to the volleyball court together. The little girl tried hard, but she missed every ball that came her way.

Watching the other campers throughout the day didn't help either. They seemed to enjoy *all* the activities.

That night all the campers climbed into their beds and fell fast asleep—all but the little girl, that is. The dark and quiet made her feel lonely, so once again she turned to her book.

"What are you doing?" whispered Jenny, the girl in the next bed. She had noticed the glow of a flashlight coming from under the little girl's blanket.

"I'm reading," said the little girl. "It helps me fall asleep. What are you doing up?"

"I guess I'm a little homesick," said Jenny softly.

"I know what you mean," said the little girl. "A good story always makes *me* feel better. What if I read to you?"

"O.K.," said Jenny, settling in beside her. And the little girl read to Jenny until they were both quite sleepy.

Things got off to an early start the next day. The little girl went from tennis to archery to canoeing to swimming. But she felt

that she wasn't good at any of them. So when volleyball was announced, the little girl slipped back to her cabin to read.

Once again the little girl became lost in her book. And once again she was surprised by her counselor.

"I've got an idea," said the counselor. "Join the group now, and I promise that tonight we'll do something you're good at. How about it?"

The little girl agreed, although she could not think of anything that she was good at.

That night after dinner, the campers gathered together for a campfire. When everyone was assembled, the counselor made an announcement.

"Usually it's my job to tell the stories, but this year we're breaking with tradition," she said. "I'd like to ask one of our new campers to read to us from one of her books," the counselor continued as she handed the little girl a book.

At first the little girl was afraid to get up in front of everyone. "But you're such a good reader!" exclaimed Jenny.

The little girl smiled shyly. Slowly she opened her book, took a deep breath and began to read. With spirit and enthusiasm, she entertained them all. She used a high-pitched voice for a silly character and a deep voice for a very serious one. And when she came to the end of one story, the campers cried, "Just one more."

The counselor smiled. "It's getting late," she said. "You'll have to wait until tomorrow night."

The next morning, things began to change for the little girl. Jenny asked to be her partner for tennis.

And they remained partners for the rest of camp. With the help of a friend, every-thing seemed easier.

Soon the little girl began to enjoy all
the daily activities. Even volleyball.

And all the campers looked forward to
the little girl's nightly story by the campfire.

Before long it was time for the last campfire. No one could believe how quickly the week had gone by. Everyone gathered together to sing and toast marshmallows and, of course, listen to the little girl read one final story in her book.

Her eyes were wide with excitement, and her voice rose and fell dramatically as she read. It was as if she had become part of the story, and everyone else became part of it too. When she finished, there was a moment of silence, and then the sound of applause. "That was the best story ever," called out one camper. "We don't want it to be over," said another.

And neither did the little girl.

The next morning an awards ceremony was held. Campers were honored for their outstanding performances in camp activities. The little girl was really surprised when her counselor called her name.

"For excellence in storytelling and for making the written word come to life," announced the counselor, "we present you with this very special award." Then she gave the little girl a miniature golden book on a golden chain. It sparkled brightly in the morning sunlight. The little girl thanked her counselor and gave her a big hug.

All her friends cheered, especially Jenny.

After the ceremony everyone went back to their cabins to pack.

Finally, it was time to say good-bye. Jenny and the little girl were sad to be leaving for they had become good friends.

"I'm going to miss you and all of your stories," Jenny told the little girl as they hugged.

"I'll miss you, too," said the little girl. "You're a great tennis coach."

"Will you write to me?" Jenny asked.

"Sure, and I'll tell you all about the new books I'm reading," added the little girl.

"See you next summer," they called to each other as they boarded their buses.

Even though the little girl missed camp, she was happy to be home again. She told her parents all about her camp adventures and about her new friend and the nightly storytelling around the campfire.

From that day on, the little girl wore her golden book charm necklace. She was proud of her award. It reminded her that she had been the heroine of her own adventure.

And always would be.

About the Author

Elizabeth Koda-Callan is a designer, illustrator and best-selling children's book author who lives in New York City. If she could go to camp now, her favorite activities would be canoeing and tennis. And, of course, reading.

She is the creator of the Magic Charm Books™ series, which includes THE MAGIC LOCKET, THE SILVER SLIPPERS, THE GOOD LUCK PONY, THE TINY ANGEL, THE SHINY SKATES, THE CAT NEXT DOOR, THE TWO BEST FRIENDS and THE QUEEN OF HEARTS.